OLD RED
Harvest

Printed in the United States of America
First Printing, 2022
ISBN 979-8-9850580-8-6

Edited by Jen Payne, Words by Jen (Branford, CT)

Sterling, Connecticut
www.artistmarnie.com

Dedicated To…

Aiden who loves a pretty red tractor!

#redinstead

And my new grandson Colton, whom
I hope will love an old red tractor too!

And everyone else who enjoys a pretty tractor!

Old Red continued to enjoy her days with her family.
Life was good.
After a busy tulip season, things slowed down for her and her family. During the summer, she carried her owner all over the farm for everyday chores.

And she enjoyed her favorite chore of all… giving rides to children. This slower time was nice, as harvest season would arrive soon, and she would be busy again!

Harvest season came in the fall when the days grew shorter, and the trees turned bright colors. The farm would open to visitors again, and there was so much to do!

Old Red loved helping with everything.
Helping others made her feel good.

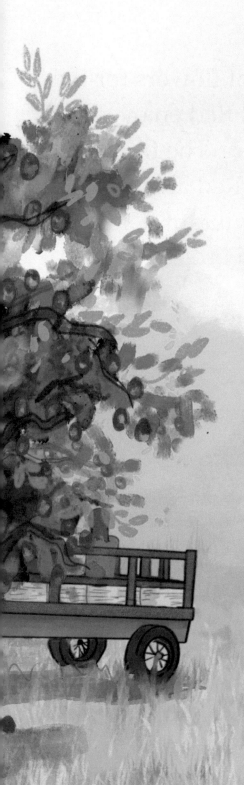

Many families visited the farm at harvest time, and Red loved pulling them once again in her wagon throughout the farm. She pulled the wagon through the large apple orchard which was filled with many different varieties of apple trees.

People enjoyed seeing glimpses of Old Red as she puttered through the rows of trees overflowing with their bright red, shiny fruit. Some even matched her own red color!

The farm recently added a field of flowers for the visitors to pick bouquets, and Red enjoyed visiting it as much as the visitors. The flowers were colorful by themselves, but Red always stole the show passing through the vibrant field of flowers that could be picked and brought home!

But Red's favorite spot to drive by was past the crop of Pinky Winkies. Pinkie Winkies were small delicate flowers that grouped together to make large blooms sometimes as big as this book!

When Red drove by them, bees flew around her, buzzing happily. The Pinkie Winkies were a glorious sight as she traveled along the dirt road.

But it wasn't just about taking visitors through the flowers, Red had to help the farm get ready, too! She helped bring pumpkins from the pumpkin patch to the farm stand, to be bought by passersby.

The day before the farm opened for the fall season, Red was parked out front as a display near the farm stand, with a sign saying they would be opening soon!

She loved being on display, and having people take photos of her as they passed by! Who knew who she might inspire…an artist or an author?

Pick your own pumpkins!
Tractor rides
THIS WEEKEND!

Or maybe just bring back memories
of a beloved family member who
also loved tractors!

Harvest season went by quickly, and Red loved every minute of it! Once it was over, her family enjoyed a well-earned rest. They spent the Thanksgiving holiday together with Red just outside the window, always a part of their days.

The next season was winter, and it was a season that was quite fickle. Fickle because some years they did not get much snow and other years they were buried in it! Living in a northern state, her owner knew that he had to prepare Red for the cold weather ahead.

Getting her ready for the cold season meant she had to be winterized. The first thing he did was check her antifreeze. Antifreeze was the coolant that flowed around her engine. And just like the word implied, the liquid did not freeze. Because if the liquid around the engine did freeze, it would crack her engine block. If this happened, Red would need a lot of repair…if she could be repaired at all.

So her owner had to make sure this liquid was in good condition for the cold weather.

To check the antifreeze strength, her owner used an antifreeze tester. He used the tester to collect some liquid from the radiator and then read the gauge to test its strength. Over time antifreeze can become diluted and will lose its strength. This time, the antifreeze measured perfectly for the cold temperatures ahead.

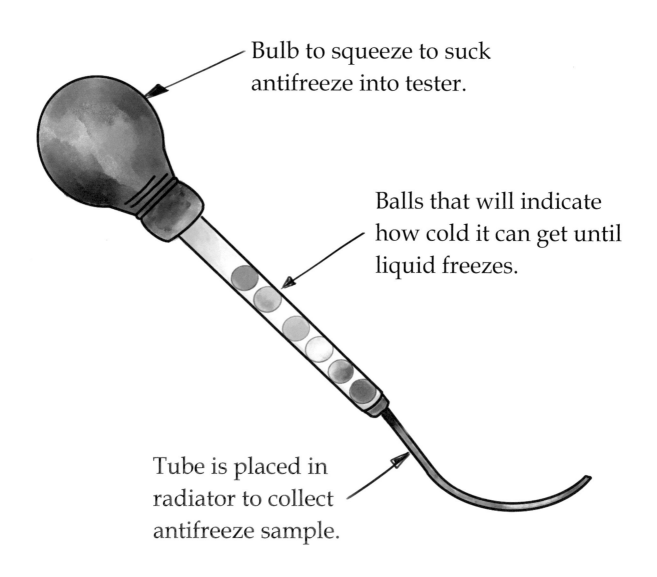

Bulb to squeeze to suck antifreeze into tester.

Balls that will indicate how cold it can get until liquid freezes.

Tube is placed in radiator to collect antifreeze sample.

Red imagined herself in disrepair and was grateful she was taken care of so well and not sitting in a barn forgotten and waiting.

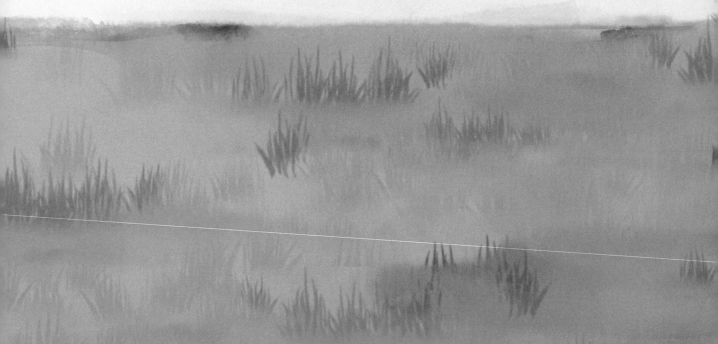

The next thing to be checked was her oil, so her owner gave Red an oil change and used a thinner oil. The thinner oil would help her run better in the cold weather.

Why does thinner oil help? Think about hot fudge… when it gets cold, it becomes a clump in your ice cream. But when the fudge is warm it flows. Oil is not as thick as fudge, but it behaves similarly. When cold oil is thick, it makes the pistons struggle to move. Thinner oil makes the pistons move easier and also helps the engine to run warmer in the cold weather. This makes a big difference on extremely cold days!

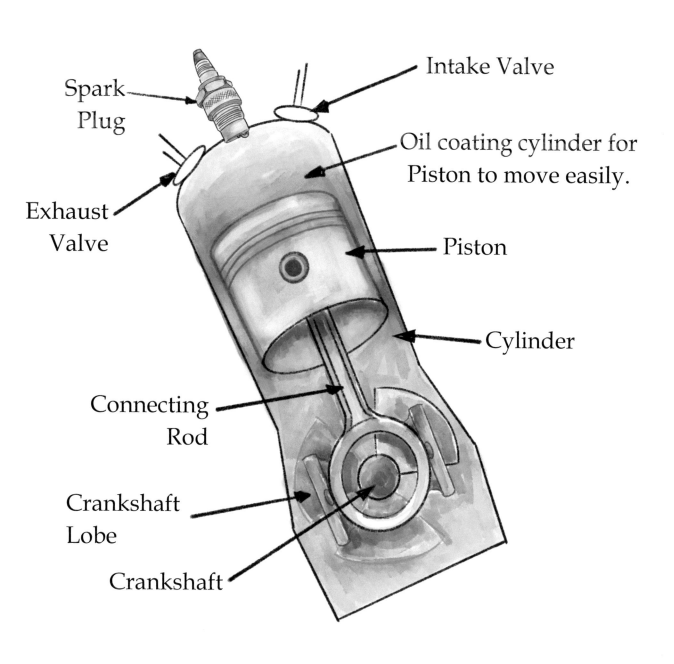

Spark
Plug

Intake Valve

Oil coating cylinder for
Piston to move easily.

Exhaust
Valve

Piston

Cylinder

Connecting
Rod

Crankshaft
Lobe

Crankshaft

Running warmer in winter was also because of a heat houser. A heat houser was fabric that covered the engine area, containing the heat. The houser kept Red and her owner warm on really frigid days.

This shroud kept the heat that the engine made surround the engine, helping to make it run smooth in extreme weather. And there was also a heat shroud for her owner too, which helped to keep him warm as well!

Red's owner looked over his list to winterize Old Red. He checked each item off as he completed it.

Checking the fluids for water, making sure connections were tight and many other tasks ensured that Red would run smoothly in the cold temperatures. Cold weather made everything run hard, and he wanted to make things easy for her…and himself too! It was not fun to work on a tractor not running well in the cold weather, and he wanted to avoid that as much as possible.

If it was forecasted to be extremely cold, he would also add an additive to her fuel, to keep the gas from freezing too!

.

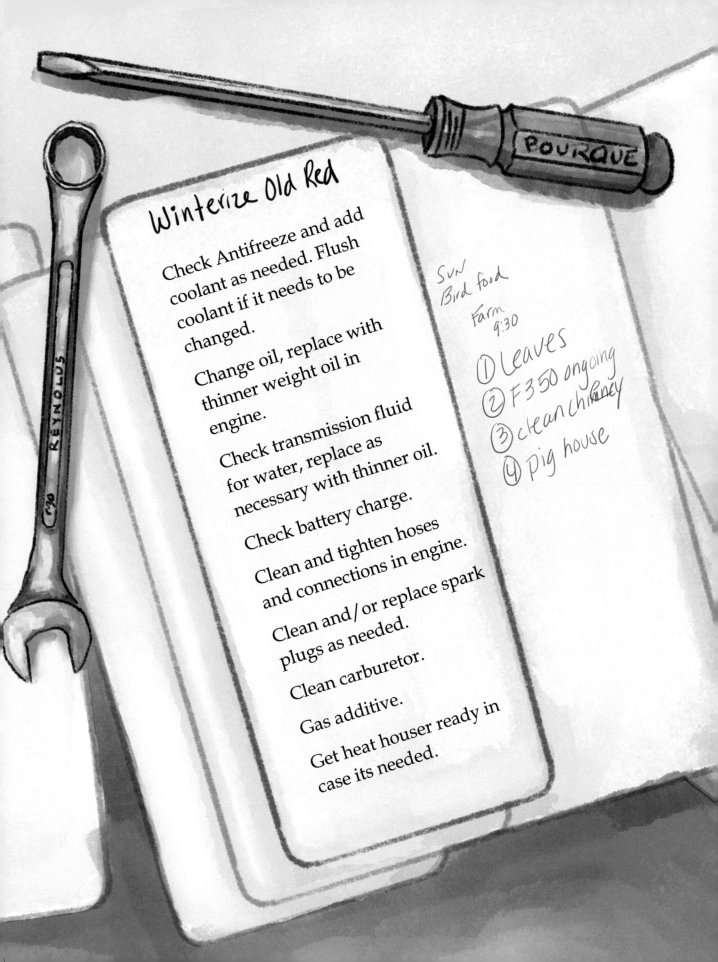

Winterize Old Red

Check Antifreeze and add coolant as needed. Flush coolant if it needs to be changed.

Change oil, replace with thinner weight oil in engine.

Check transmission fluid for water, replace as necessary with thinner oil.

Check battery charge.

Clean and tighten hoses and connections in engine.

Clean and/or replace spark plugs as needed.

Clean carburetor.

Gas additive.

Get heat houser ready in case its needed.

Sun
Bird food
Farm
9:30

① Leaves
② F350 ongoing
③ clean chimney
④ pig house

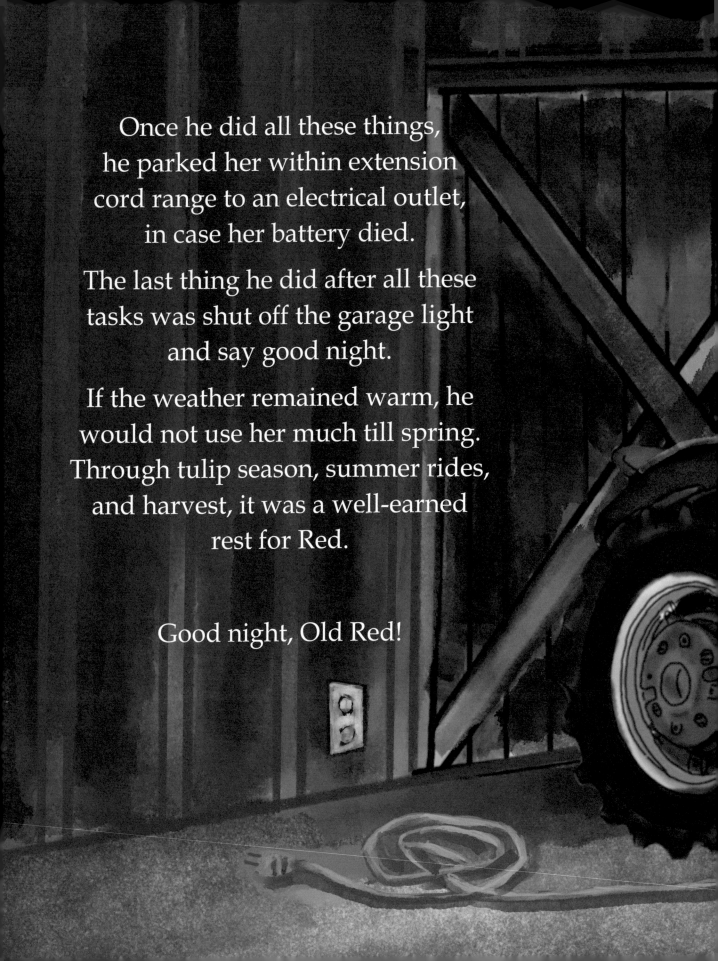

Once he did all these things,
he parked her within extension
cord range to an electrical outlet,
in case her battery died.

The last thing he did after all these
tasks was shut off the garage light
and say good night.

If the weather remained warm, he
would not use her much till spring.
Through tulip season, summer rides,
and harvest, it was a well-earned
rest for Red.

Good night, Old Red!

Thank you for reading my book! When not writing or illustrating, I am painting and dreaming of traveling with my loved ones. I have a website, artistmarnie.com, where you can see more of my colorful, happy work.

Marnie

My other books are:

Discover where your cousins live with a map of the USA and learn about family with somebushy-tailed squirrels and then fill out a family tree together!

A sentimental tale of tending flowers with mom, daughter and then granddaughter. Learn about flowers and how life goes on after empty nest.

Old Red's Adventures... colorful stories about a restored tractor on her farm.

Observe and learn to appreciate the little things, while enjoying illustrations of Beavertail lighthouse in Jamestown, Rhode Island.

Enjoy the story of an antique car, and learn about combustion engines and the differences between modern cars and a Model A!

Learn why animals may be near the road, and instill a compassion in your children for wildlife.

Read all about how much aunties love their family, and how to show you love them in return.

A tale about making bath time fun and stimulating children's imagination.

Observe a kitty growing up in a shelter, and learn how shelters help animals in need! 100% of profits from book go to Paws Cat Shelter, in Woodstock, CT.

Made in United States
Troutdale, OR
10/10/2024